LITTLE MISS
SHY
and the Lion

Roger Hargreaves

MR. MEN   **LITTLE MISS**

MR. MEN™ LITTLE MISS™ © THOIP (a SANRIO company)

Little Miss Shy and the Lion © 2014 THOIP (a SANRIO company)
Printed and published under licence from Price Stern Sloan, Inc., Los Angeles.
First published in France 1997 by Hachette Livre
This edition published in 2015 by Dean, an imprint of Egmont UK Limited,
The Yellow Building, 1 Nicholas Road, London W11 4AN

ISBN 978 0 6035 7001 8
58241/2
Printed in Great Britain

EGMONT

Poor Little Miss Shy was terribly, desperately shy. She lived all alone in a little cottage, far away from everyone.

Every time she left her cottage she checked to be sure that nobody was around.

Without a doubt, there was no one else in the world as shy as Little Miss Shy.

At least, that's what she thought.

Little Miss Shy was so very shy that she even blushed when she looked in the mirror.

She blushed like a beetroot!

Can you imagine being that shy?

One day a circus arrived in the village.

Little Miss Shy wished she could go, but there would be people there – how terrifying! And animals – even more terrifying!

Little Miss Shy decided she would rather spend the day under her bedcovers.

"Quickly! Give me a ticket. I am in a great hurry," said Mr Rush, arriving at the circus. "I've come to see Leonardo, the amazing performing lion, and then I must rush. So much to do."

Just then a clown ran up.

"Help! Help! The lion has escaped!" he shouted.

"I wish you'd told me sooner," said Mr Rush. "I could have saved myself some time."

"Oh dear," worried Mr Bump.

But Leonardo was not a fierce lion. He was a shy lion. So shy, in fact, that he had run away from the circus because he didn't want to stand in front of the audience.

He was so very, very shy.

It wasn't long before Leonardo came to the cottage of Little Miss Shy. Shyly, he peeped in the window and he was happy to see that Little Miss Shy was fast asleep.

He spent the night in the garden.

The next morning Little Miss Shy found a letter on the doorstep.

Who could it be from?

She was in such a hurry to read it that she forgot to shut the door behind her.

The lion crept into the house!

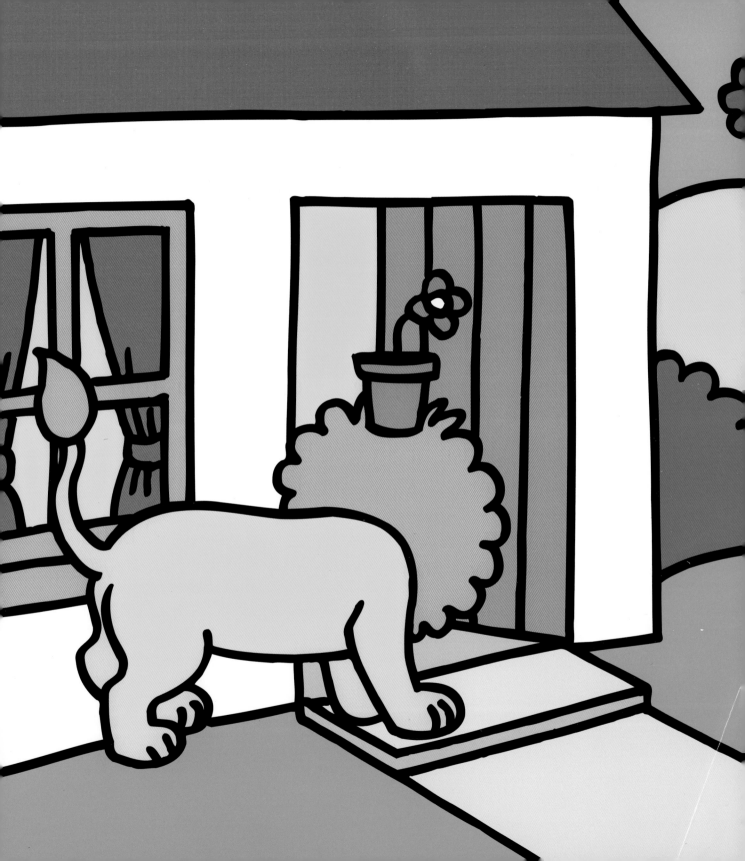

The letter said:

RUNAWAY LION!
Our very shy, performing lion, Leonardo, has run away from the circus.
If you see him please bring him back.
He wears a flower upon his head.

"Performing in front of an audience!" squealed Little Miss Shy. "The poor lion! No wonder he ran away."

Purrr …. Purrr….

Little Miss Shy turned around and there, just behind her chair, was Leonardo, the shy lion!

Once she had got over her shock she felt terribly shy. But then she remembered that Leonardo was also shy.

Was it possible that he could be more shy than her?

Little Miss Shy bravely invited the lion into her kitchen and bravely he accepted.

Knock! Knock!

"Let me in," came the loud voice of the ringmaster. "I hear that my lion has been seen near your house."

"Don't worry," Little Miss Shy whispered to the lion. "I'm here to look after you."

With newfound bravery, Little Miss Shy opened the door and shouted, "How could you! Forcing such a shy lion to perform! He is going to stay here and live with me."

Little Miss Shy had completely forgotten her own shyness!

The ringmaster was forced to agree that the circus wasn't the best place for a shy lion like Leonardo.

Mr Rush and Mr Bump, who had followed the ringmaster, were amazed to hear Little Miss Shy shouting. They had never even heard her whisper.

They rushed up and gave Little Miss Shy and then Leonardo enormous hugs.

And they both blushed as red as a whole bag of beetroots!